SAMUEL MARSHAK

THE ABSENTMINDED FELLOW

Translated from the Russian by Richard Pevear

Pictures by Marc Rosenthal

Farrar, Straus and Giroux   New York

Library of Congress Cataloging-in-Publication Data
Marshak, S. (Samuil), 1887–1964.
   [Vot kakoĭ Rasseyanniĭ. English]
   The absentminded fellow / Samuel Marshak ; translated from
the Russian by Richard Pevear ; pictures by Marc Rosenthal.
      p.   cm.
   "This translation is an adaptation of 'Vot kakoi Rasseyannii'."
   Summary: From the time he puts his pants on his arms until he tries
to buy a train ticket at the flower shop, "that absentminded fellow
from Portobello Road" bumbles from one muddle to the next.
   ISBN 0-374-30013-5
   [1. Humorous stories. 2. Stories in rhyme.]   I. Pevear, Richard.
II. Rosenthal, Marc, 1949–   ill.   III. Title.
PZ8.3.M394Ab   1999
[E]—dc21   98-22890

To Milton Glaser
M.R.

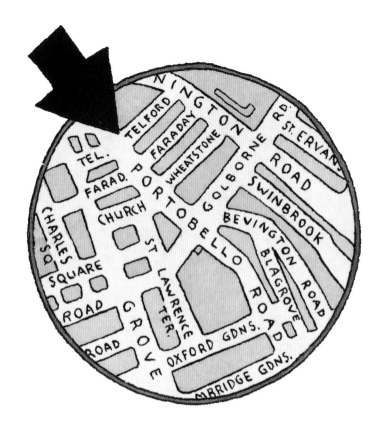

An absentminded fellow
Lived on Portobello Road.

He woke up one morning,
Took his trousers from the chair,
Stuck his arms through the legs
And waved them in the air . . .

With his feet through his sleeves
He came out to the hall.
As he headed for the stairway,
We said, "Look out, you'll fall!"

He was never quite certain
What, which, or whether,
And when he tied his shoes
He tied them to each other.

He threw on his overcoat.
We said, "It isn't yours!"
Then he opened his umbrella
Before he went outdoors.

That morning he was rushing
To catch an evening train.
He jumped into a taxi:

At last the weary taxi
Dropped our fellow at the station.
He dashed into a flower shop
To make a reservation.

He rushed along the platform
And found an empty car.

He woke up the next morning.
The station was astir.

"What stop is this?" he called out.
"The city of London, sir."

He leaned back, put his feet up,
And slept a little more.

He woke up: "What's this station?"
"The city of London, sir."

He slept again, woke up again,
Thought now he *must* be there.

"Is this Birmingham?" he shouted.
"The city of London, sir!"

"London, London, London . . . ?"
Our fellow scratched his head.

"I was going to Birmingham,
But I came back instead!"